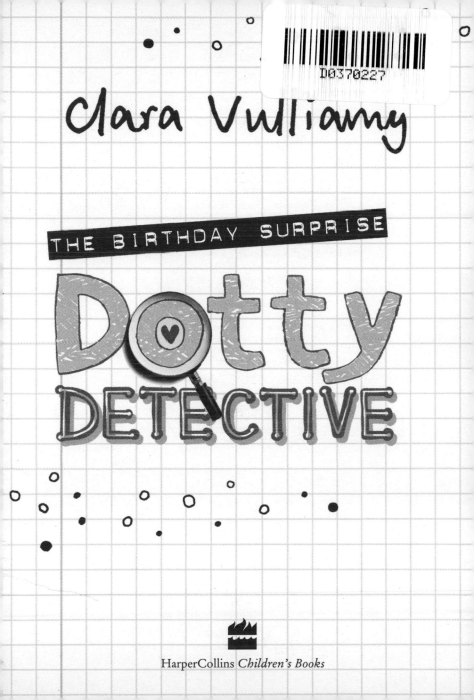

Clara Vulliamy

THE BIRTHDAY SURPRISE

Dotty DETECTIVE

HarperCollins *Children's Books*

First published in Great Britain by
HarperCollins *Children's Books* in 2018
First published in the United States of America in this edition by
HarperCollins *Children's Books* 2019
HarperCollins *Children's Books* is a division of
HarperCollins*Publishers* Ltd,
HarperCollins Publishers
1 London Bridge Street
London SE1 9GF

The HarperCollins website address is:
www.harpercollins.co.uk

1

ISBN 978-0-00-830090-6

Printed and bound by
CPI Group (UK) Ltd, Croydon, CR0 4YY

MIX
Paper from
responsible sources
FSC™ C007454

For Melanie, Eva, and Claudia,
with much love

Read the whole series:

★ *Dotty Detective*

★ *Dotty Detective: The Pawprint Puzzle*

★ *Dotty Detective: The Midnight Mystery*

★ *Dotty Detective: The Lost Puppy*

★ *Dotty Detective: The Birthday Surprise*

Coming soon:

★*Dotty Detective: The Vacation Mystery*

This book
belongs to . . .

DOT

and McClusky

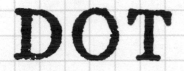

This is me—Dot!

I live with Mom, the twins (my
brother and sister, Alf and Maisy),
and my **crazy** dog, McClusky.

It's *noodles* for dinner, which is my *absolute* favorite, but I can hardly concentrate...

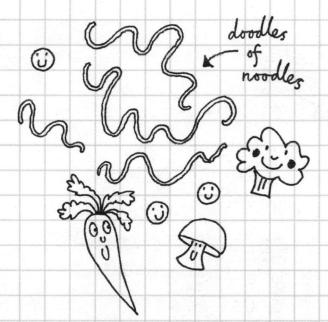

doodles of noodles

because I am too *utterly totally incredibly* **MASSIVELY** excited...

My birthday is in exactly TWO WEEKS! And tonight I'm making my **party invitations**.

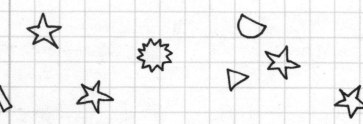

The twins' birthday is in August and for their last party we had a picnic in the park with Popsicles and a machine that **blows bᵤbᵦles**.

We don't know when McClusky's birthday is because he's a rescue dog,

so each year
he has THREE
birthday parties
(just in
case he didn't
have enough
special celebrations
before he became
part of our
family).

But when it comes to MY party, I am *completely* in the dark. Mom refuses to tell me anything about what she is planning.

Even when I say, "**Please, please, PLEASE**—just give me ONE tiny clue!" she does the zip-the-lips gesture.

"My lips are sealed," she says.

Bedtime. This might look like just an ordinary bedroom, but OH NO.

I have something EXTREMELY important to tell you ...

Me, my best friend—Beans —, and McClusky are super-secret, super-sleuthing DETECTIVES!

JOIN THE DOTS DETECTIVES

13

And my bedroom is our HQ.

This is where we study the clues and piece together the evidence. However murky the mystery or fiendishly tricky the puzzle, together we always solve the case.

??

But at the moment the **biggest** mystery in my life is—what will my birthday party be?

Roller-disco? Go-karting? Will there be a magician?

I make party invitations for all my friends with my **awesome** stationery collection.

Woo-HOOO! I can use my new clock stamp to show the times!

I'm pretty happy with the result ...

MONDAY

Mom is calling,

"HURRY UP! WE'RE GOING TO BE LATE FOR SCHOOL!"

I'm already standing by the front door ready to leave; but the twins are running up and down the hall,

wearing their school sweaters
like capes, and pretending
to be

SUPERHEROES.

They ALWAYS make us need to rush.

Arriving at school there is only JUST time to say hello to the **school-gate gang**, McClusky's dog friends.

They wait together outside school at drop-off and dismissal, because they aren't allowed into the playground.

I reach up to pat big Geoffrey, and reach down to stroke little sausage dog puppy, Chorizo.
Her ears are SO soft.

Hurrying over to line up and hand out my party invitations and—oh!—there's a NEW BOY I've never seen before.

At attendance, our teacher, Mr. Dickens, says, "Listen up, everybody! Let's all give a HUGE, friendly welcome to Bradley, who has just joined our class!"

We all call out, **"HI!"** **"HEY!"** **"YAY!"** **"HOLA!"** **"HOWDY!"** until Frankie gets carried away with this huge, friendly welcome and falls off his chair.

"Tell us a bit about yourself, Bradley," says Mr. D.

"Well, for a start, I am good at **LOTS** of things!" says Bradley. He shows us his achievement badges—football captain, school council, spelling bee award, outstanding student . . .

They are all bright red, the color of his old school, not our school colors, which are yellow and blue.

Bradley sits on the table next to ours, right behind Beans.

Me and Beans are chatting about my **party mystery**. I see Bradley watching us.

I'm just in the middle of my list of guesses, but Bradley **interrupts** by *tapping* Beans on the shoulder and starts talking to him.

While we are supposed to be sorting out the pen jars, Bradley wants to show Beans his shiny red *STAR STUDENT* pencil case. Beans is very impressed.

I remember being the new person in class and not knowing anyone at first, so I try not to mind.

And now Mr. D. is saying, "I have an *announcement*!" and doing his

exciting news dance.

"Today we will start our Ancient Egypt project! There will be lots of fun stuff like a trip to the museum and a big art display in the hall for the rest of the school to admire . . . and next Friday will be

EGYPT DAY

when we will all dress up—which will be extra special because it is also the same day as MY BIRTHDAY!"

Amazing!

TWO birthdays only two days apart—mine and Mr. D.'s!

Now Mr. D. is drawing **balloons** and birthday cakes around the date of his birthday on the classroom wall calendar.

FRIDAY
9th

When Mr. D. is happy, he makes up silly songs.

"I can hardly wait! It will be so great! Hip hip hip hoorays! Counting down the days!" he sings.

He is easily as **excited** about his birthday as I am about mine—which is *so funny* because he is a grown-up!

Breaktime. Beans goes off with Bradley, but that's fine as I am busy eating my Cheesy Wheat Crunchers and having a

bright

idea . . .

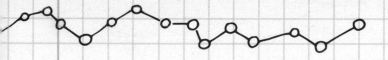

In class while Mr. D. is distracted in the stationery cupboard, I whisper my idea to my friends . . .

"Let's do something *really special* for Mr. D.'s birthday," I say, "and make a wonderful surprise present for him!" They think this is GREAT!

We all do secret **high fives** under the table.

"I'm **too excited** to wait—
I'll start making it tonight!" I tell
them. "Everyone, bring in your best
stickers and **glitter** and **decorations**
tomorrow!"

In Geography we are drawing maps of **Ancient Egypt** for the class display in the hall.

Beans, who is *amazing* at maps, is in a pair with Bradley.

Me and Fiyaz do our best with some yellow and blue pencils. The Red Sea looks like a **weird** rabbit and our camels are a *bit* funny, so we mainly draw lots of sand dunes instead.

Back at home, *super-speedily* having my dinner so I can rush to Dot HQ...

 I think I have the PERFECT thing for Mr. D.'s special present!

Rummaging in my shoebox of extra-precious treasures . . .

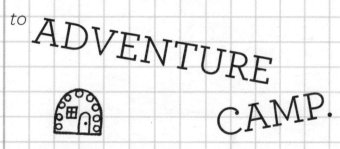

Here it is—a photo from our school trip to ADVENTURE CAMP.

We are all in it—me, Beans, Amy, Joe, Fiyaz, Frankie, Nadia, and Kirstie—and Mr. D. is in the middle with a huge smile on his face. I make a card frame for it, and decorate around the edge with glittery pens, pom-poms, and birthday stickers.

He is going to absolutely **LOVE** it!

Tuesday

Rushing to line up with Mr. D.'s present safely in my bag ... Beans is already here, chatting to Bradley.

Beans is showing him his shiny new **ten-sided dice**. I REALLY want to see too, but Bradley turns his back on me so my view is blocked.

It takes AGES to find a good moment to show everyone Mr. D.'s present . . .

But at breaktime it's wet play, which is REALLY LUCKY! While Mr. D. is distracted by dunking a cookie into his coffee and trying to fish it out again . . .

BEST
TEACHER

I secretly show my group of friends the photo in the collaged frame.

All together we add the extra decorations brought in from home. Joe has **sparkly rainbow glitter**, Nadia has brought in tiny **pearl buttons** and Fiyaz has filled his pocket with different colored **sequins**.

It's looking AMAZING!

Beans joins in with some pieces of nice stripy string he finds at the bottom of his bag. But Bradley makes a sulky face so Beans goes off to sit with him instead.

In Math we are making a sugar-cube pyramid for the **EGYPT** display.

This is how we do it . . .

4 rows of 12 sugar cubes arranged in a square . . .

then 4 rows of 11 sugar cubes stepped in slightly and glued into place...

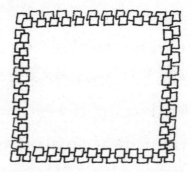

the same with 4 rows of 10

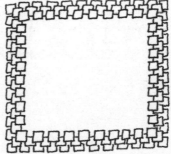

and repeat until there is just one on the top!

Mr. D. tells us about the pharaoh's burial chambers and the **SECRETS OF THE GREAT PYRAMIDS**.

"Imagine—caskets of treasure hidden behind **locked** doors along cramped, dusty corridors, undiscovered for

THOUSANDS

of

years!"

he says.

At dismissal we put the finishing touches on Mr. D.'s special surprise present, and Joe adds one last handful of **glitter** for **extra sparkle**.

We all write birthday messages on the back.

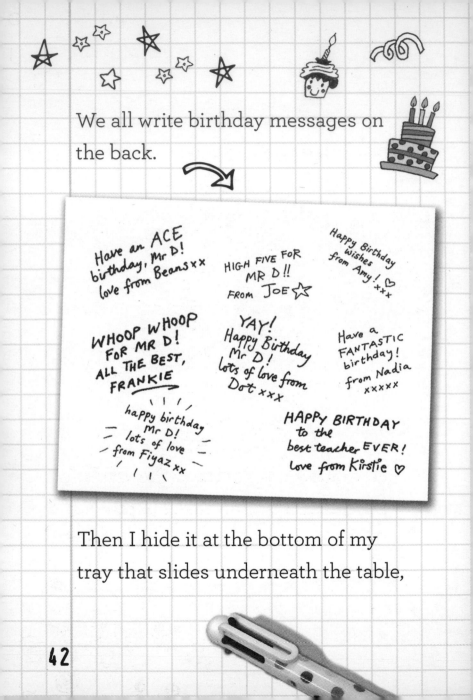

Have an ACE birthday, Mr D! love from Beans xx

HIGH FIVE FOR MR D !! FROM JOE ☆

Happy Birthday wishes from Amy ! ♡ xxx

WHOOP WHOOP FOR MR D! ALL THE BEST, FRANKIE

YAY! Happy Birthday Mr D! lots of love from Dot xxx

Have a FANTASTIC birthday! from Nadia xxxxx

happy birthday Mr D! lots of love from Fizgaz xx

HAPPY BIRTHDAY to the best teacher EVER! love from Kirstie ♡

Then I hide it at the bottom of my tray that slides underneath the table, buried under a pile of things that I keep there.

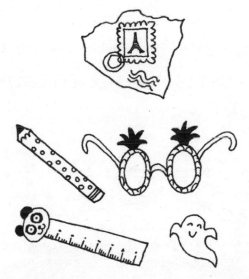

At home, clearing the dishes after supper and feeling really happy . . . This is going to be an EXTRA-good evening!

Cozy on the sofa under my best polka-dot blanket, mug of hot chocolate, watching my favorite TV program EVER, which is **FRED FANTASTIC—ACE DETECTIVE**.

There are many **dastardly** villains on the mean streets of the big city, up to no good. It's down to detectives Fred and his cool sidekick, Flo, to put a stop to them.

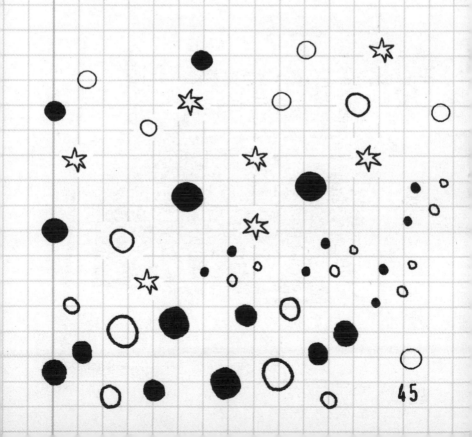

And now that Mr. D.'s present is finished *PHEW* I can concentrate on writing *my own* birthday-present list!

red sneakers

glow-in-the-dark paperclips

polka-dot stickers

Fred and Flo's Fantastically Fab Storybook

polka-dot socks

change-color umbrella

Pony

WednesDay

Coming into class at attendance,
I just want to **admire** Mr. D.'s present
again. Rummaging down to the
bottom of my tray . . .

I CAN'T SEE IT!

Frantically searching again . . .
The special present

has

DISAPPEARED.

This is a

DISASTER!

I MUST find it before anyone else realizes it's gone and starts a *panic*.

While everyone bustles to and fro to move places for English, I secretly peep inside the other trays at my table. Could it have been moved *by mistake*?

Beans keeps a **huge** collection
of rubber bands in his tray, Frankie
has a *very old* apple core and lots
of important unopened school letters
he never took home and Amy has
the neatest, tidiest tray I have EVER
seen . . .

But NO—no sign of Mr. D.'s present.

Everyone is heading out into the playground for breaktime. Now's my chance for a bigger search! I pretend I've forgotten my water bottle and *hurry* back to the classroom.

I check the stationery cupboard,
the lunchbox crates,
the shelves ...
but

NO SIGN.

At lunchtime I'm feeling **too stressed** to eat more than *one bite* of my sandwich . . .

and even **more stressed** when everyone starts asking me about my party!

"What sort of party will it be?" asks Kirstie.

"Tell us, Dot!" says Fiyaz.

"It's a **SECRET!**" I say. "I am keeping it **UNDER MY HAT.**"

I smile *mysteriously* and just hope that nobody guesses I have **no idea!**

Usually I would talk to Beans about this, but he is sitting at a different table, eating his lunch with Bradley.

To make matters **EVEN WORSE,** Laura (who is *not* always my favorite person, I can tell you) starts talking about all the amazing super-fancy parties she has had.

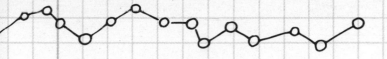

"Once a bunch of us went to the theater and the tickets were *really* expensive and afterwards we went to the BEST restaurant. And another time I had a **spa pamper party** and we put our feet in a bucket of cucumber and—"

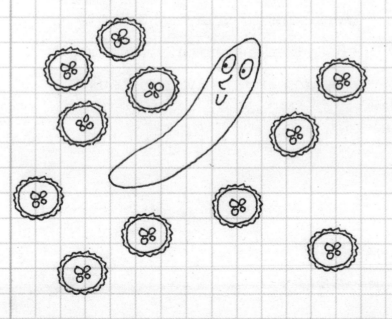

But I've stopped listening. This is making me feel uneasy. I'm pretty sure that putting my feet in a bucket of cucumber ISN'T my idea of the perfect party, but I wish I DID know what Mom is planning!

At dismissal when everyone is distracted by packing their bags, I search around the coat hooks ... but

NOTHING.

Lying on my bed, thinking about Mr. D.'s missing present...

And worrying.

There's no avoiding it: I must tell the others in the morning.

Thursday

As soon as we get into the classroom, I beckon my friends into a huddle and whisper, "It's *gone*—Mr. D.'s special present is **MISSING!**"

They GASP in *horror*.

"EXTREMELY *mysterious!*" says Beans, catching my eye. I know *exactly* what he is thinking—this is just the kind of **puzzle** me and Beans are so good at solving!

"Have you searched everywhere?" asks Amy.

"High and low?" adds Joe.

"I have looked EVERYWHERE I can think of . . ." I tell them.

"A-HA!" says a voice behind us. It's Bradley—he has been eavesdropping and heard everything! "You may have looked everywhere *you* can think of," he says, "but it will take an **amazing** detective like ME to find it!"

Me and Beans look at each other in utter bewilderment. Together we have secretly solved the **trickiest** cases and the MURKIEST OF MYSTERIES. And now Bradley thinks HE is a detective too!

I realize Bradley is watching. I am just about to say something to Beans, but Bradley interrupts.

"I know," he says, "let's make it a boys-against-girls detective race to find the present—and see who finds it first. I bet the BOYS will win!"

I can see Beans hesitating, but Bradley bossily rounds up his team. So I gather mine together too.

59

The girls' team is Kirstie, me, Amy, and Nadia. The boys' team is Joe, Frankie, Bradley, Beans, and Fiyaz.

THE CASE OF THE MISSING BIRTHDAY PRESENT has begun—and it's *Girl Detectives versus Boy Detectives!*

"This case will be a piece
of cake—SO EASY!"
Bradley says to his team.

"We need to keep searching, and look
for clues . . ." I say to my team.

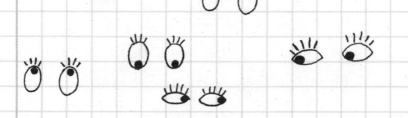

We look again in all the same places.
I might have missed something . . .
BUT NO LUCK.

"Maybe it wasn't *accidentally* lost?"
I say. It's all starting to look very
suspicious...

We are just heading over to the
library when Bradley says,
"Dot, YOU must have deliberately
hidden the present *yourself*!"
He is pointing triumphantly.
"You have glitter on your
hands! LOOK!"

It's true, I do, BUT...

"So do YOU, Bradley!" I say.

Kirstie adds, "And what about Joe?
He even has glitter in his HAIR!"

We are ALL a bit **glittery!** Ever since
Joe brought in his rainbow glitter, it
has gone pretty much everywhere.
So the glitter *isn't* a clue after all.

We hurry over to the farthest bookshelves to choose our books, but *really* we are discussing the case. "We need to think about **SUSPECTS**," I say.

"Who could have got into the classroom before school starts in the morning?" Nadia wonders.

"I know!" says Amy. "It must be someone in the **Breakfast Club!**

But WHO?"

"Ace detective work, team!" I say.
"We MUST get a look at the
Breakfast Club list . . ."

Back in class we saunter *extremely*
casually past Mr. D.'s desk, but the
clubs book is closed. Mr. D. raises
an eyebrow at us.

Heading out to lunch, I see the book is open! This could be my chance!

I saunter backwards past Mr. D.'s desk ... but

AAARGH

it's open to the Chess Club page!

Mr. D. raises the other eyebrow.

In the afternoon we are learning about hieroglyphs, which is **Ancient Egyptian** picture writing.

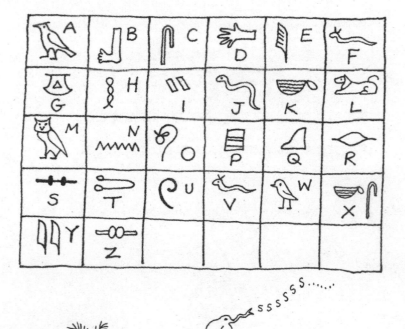

Interesting fact—a hieroglyphic word can be written **right to left** *or* **left to right**. You can tell which way it should be read because the humans or animals *always* face toward the beginning of the word.

We practice writing our names.
I write McClusky's name too—but backwards!

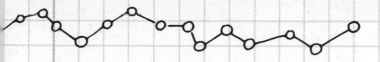

At dismissal, the clubs book is open on the right page.

AT LAST

I see the Breakfast Club list...

In the chaos of the playground, I can't find Nadia, Amy, or Kirstie to tell them about my discovery.

Back at home, I finish my spaghetti hoops *super-speedily*, and rush to Dot HQ...

I write a note to the rest of the girls' team using hieroglyphs.

Laura

must be up to her

old tricks

AGAIN!

FRIDAY

I carefully hide my hieroglyph note inside my library book before we go off on the walk to school.

In class, hanging up my coat and unpacking my bag, I'm waiting for the right moment to secretly slip the note to the other girl detectives . . .

But—**DISASTER**—the note falls out of my book onto the floor and—

EEEeeeEEK

—without realizing Frankie steps on it and it is STUCK TO HIS SHOE!!

Frankie walks over to his place and I *hurry* after him. But just as I reach down to grab the note . . .

Fiyaz picks it up, folds it into a paper
airplane and sends it—

WHEEEEE!

—across the room
and it is caught—OH NO!—
by Bradley!

He puts it in his pocket.

DRAT!

NO CHANCE to speak to Amy,
Nadia, or Kirstie *all morning*—Bradley
is hovering nearby all the time!

Usually I go to Knitting Club with Beans at Friday lunchtime, but I haven't seen him much this week so I don't think I will go today.

After lunch, we go over to the computer lab to research facts about a desert animal. I choose a jerboa— they are so cute and hop like a tiny kangaroo!

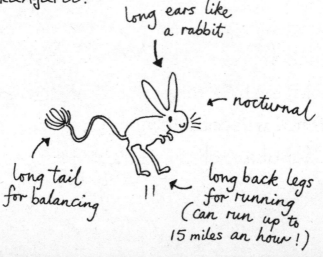

long ears like a rabbit

nocturnal

long tail for balancing

long back legs for running (can run up to 15 miles an hour!)

I am sitting next to Laura which is an unexpected opportunity to investigate **THE MAIN SUSPECT!**

"So, Laura," I ask in a casual, roundabout way, "what sort of things do you eat at Breakfast Club?"

"Oh, I haven't been to Breakfast Club for WEEKS—I have been practicing violin at home before school instead. My violin exam is very soon—I will definitely do **fabulously!**"

So it couldn't have been Laura after all. It was a *red herring*, which isn't anything to do with fish—it means that this clue led us down the wrong path.

I finish my jerboa facts, and wonder what our next move should be.

Bradley leans back in his chair and puts his hands behind his head.

"I'm feeling **GOOD** about **solving** this case *very soon!*"

"Bradley is a *really* good detective!" Beans says to me.

I don't say anything. After all the cases me and Beans have solved together, this makes me feel a bit sad.

At dismissal, Mr. D. gives out letters reminding us about the museum trip on Monday, and asking if we have any dolls at home we no longer want … "AND don't forget it's dressing up for **EGYPT DAY** next Friday!" he says. "Have a fab weekend, everybody!"

Saturday

We take McClusky for a walk in the park even though it's raining.

I think about the case while we splash through puddles—thank goodness I am wearing my polka-dot boots!

Bradley seems so sure he will find
the missing present first. What does
the boys' team know

THAT WE DON'T?

On the way home, Mom asks,
"Should we stop at Beans's house?
See if he would like to come over?"

Since Bradley arrived at our school,
Beans hasn't had much time for me.
Would he *even want* to come over?

"Not today, thanks, Mom," I say.

After lunch, to distract myself from worrying about the case, I think about my birthday instead.

ONLY EIGHT DAYS TO GO!

I design my **ideal birthday cake**. It is pink cake with white icing, and

I can't decide between sugar beans or jazzies so I add BOTH. On top there are four upside-down ice-cream cones with little flags flying. It looks like a **crazy** polka-dot castle!

I put the drawing up on the fridge with my biggest and best magnet so Mom will notice it.

I try to find out more from Mom about my party too, but she seems to have forgotten all about it! "What party?" she says. "Oh, *that* party..."

Now this is WORRYING TOO. Will it be a **big** flop?

Sunday

Mom says she is **VERY BUSY** this morning and asks if we can help with some household chores in the kitchen.

I sort the paper in the recycling box and the twins have a try with the dustpan and brush. Alf holds the dustpan and Maisy brushes, but they don't *quite* have the knack ...

there is a trail of Doggylicious
dog-biscuit crumbs
EVERYWHERE!

Mom takes McClusky into her room.

When he comes back, he is VERY
excited and I glimpse a piece of gold
thread on his ear.

WHAT

IS

GOING

ON?

MONDAY

Today it's the museum trip! Mom gives me some spending money for the shop, and I put it carefully in my **panda purse**.

Immediately after attendance it's time to go. I am in a pair with Joe to walk to the museum. Bradley and Beans are walking behind us.

"I'm really looking forward to your party!" says Joe. "I LOVE birthdays."

"Are you inviting BOYS as well as girls to your party, Dot?" says Bradley. "Girls' parties are STUPID."

"*Of course* boys are invited to my party!" I say. "Why wouldn't they be?"

Bradley *scowls*. Does he think that boys hanging out with girls is mixing with the enemy?

CRAZY!

In the museum we learn all about the different **EGYPTIAN GODS**.

HORUS   ANUBIS   THOTH   ISIS

We see a REAL mummy in an open sarcophagus, which is a stone coffin from **ancient times**, and a turquoise statue of a hippopotamus, and we even see a

MUMMIFIED CAT!!!

We all love the grisly facts about mummification.

Actually not *quite* all—Laura, who is squeamish, hurries past the jar with a baboon head on top and mummified lungs inside.

There's also a **cool** model showing the inside of a pyramid, with

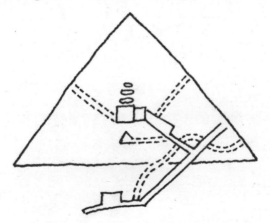

secret passages and **hiding places**.

Eating our packed lunches, Mr. D. says, "Today should be giving you lots of good ideas for your **Egyptian costumes** on Friday!"

EEK!

I haven't thought of **anything** yet!

I **love** dressing up.

Once, me and Beans went to a costume party as a

TWO-HEADED MONSTER

in one of my mom's big coats.

I look over and see Beans and Bradley pretending to be mummies and

collapsing into giggles.

I miss Beans.

It's dismissal when we arrive back at school. In fact, Mom is already in the playground waiting for me.

The girls' detective team hasn't had any chance to work on the case today. We MUST make up for lost time tomorrow!

For dinner we make **funny-face** baked potatoes. Mine has cucumber and peas for eyes, tomato for the nose and mouth, and cress for the hair!

TUEsdAy

Mr. D. is talking excitedly about his birthday. "I can hardly sleep!" he says.

This makes me and the girls' team worry *even more* about his missing present.

"Fingers crossed for a LUCKY BREAK in the case today!" I say.

"Have you ever wondered what the **Ancient Egyptians** did for their birthdays?" Mr. D. carries on.

"The pharaoh in **3000 BC** had the *first ever* mentioned birthday party in history. But it was the ANCIENT GREEKS who first put *candles* on birthday cakes!"

In Art we each make a **sarcophagus** out of cardboard and decorate them with **Egyptian patterns**.

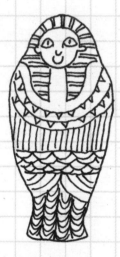

We take our **sarcophagi** over to the hall to add to the display. I'm just putting mine in a good position when I notice something ...

That's odd. What's a tiny **pearl button** doing here? I pop it in my pocket.

We are heading outside for recess. Bradley, who has gone out first, says *very loudly*

"LOOK!"

He is pointing **dramatically** toward a *small trail* of sequins leading across the playground.

He is acting like a **GREAT** detective, studying the sequins, staring into the distance, and then *writing something* in his notebook.

The other boys are standing around not doing much. I have noticed that Bradley doesn't **share** a lot with his team.

I *speedily* gather the girls' team into a huddle. "The missing present must have been hidden somewhere OUTSIDE!" I say.

"Let's split up into twos," says Kirstie.

"That way, we can cover more ground."

We search **every corner** of the playground ...

And again at lunchtime ... But it leads to

nothing.

Another **dead end**.

Arriving home, the first thing I see when I walk in through the front door is a huge MYSTERIOUS object under a sheet. There is a sign taped to it in Mom's writing.

This is *extremely* puzzling!

After dinner I watch a **FRED FANTASTIC** episode in which Fred is struggling to solve a case without Flo.

It makes me think about the

Case of the Missing Birthday Present ...

I have a GREAT team, but I'm finding this mystery *so much trickier* without Beans on my side too—he would know what to do next.

* * * * * * * *

This girls-against-boys thing is

SILLY.

Me and Beans—like Fred and Flo—are
a **very cool team** and always work
best together!

WEDNESDAY

Today we are using the unwanted dolls brought in from home to make our mummies!

They are a
STRANGE
selection.

Frankie has brought in Cynthia and tells us, "I used to take her *everywhere* when I was little until both her eyes fell out and one leg fell off—now she's *Cynthia the zombie doll!*"

Bradley says, "UGH! What **BOYS** have **DOLLS?**" and laughs. Beans laughs too.

Beans has been acting differently since Bradley arrived.

Usually on Wednesday morning, me and Beans talk about last night's episode of **FRED FANTASTIC** because he loves it too, but I don't think I want to today.

We are cutting lengths of bandage to wrap around our mummies. This gives me a **super** idea for a new way to send a message—**MUMMY MAIL!**

When no one is looking, I write a **loooooong** message to the other girl detectives on the back of a piece of bandage ...

ONLY TWO DAYS LEFT! WHERE IS THE PRESENT?

But

DISASTER!

My message is *scooped up* with the other pieces of bandage, and too soon it is wrapped around a mummy and glued into place before they can read it.

WHO IS HIDING IT ???

AGAIN I cannot get a message to the rest of my team!

To make matters worse, Bradley is always teasing us. "You seem to be getting NOWHERE!" he says. "But *I* have discovered a **VERY** important clue."

He makes a big show of writing in his notebook.

I am SO worried. Mr. D.'s present is still missing—the whole thing was my idea and it all feels like my fault. And it's too late to find something else to give him.

We have tied ourselves up in knots. Fred Fantastic says this a lot. It doesn't mean you are actually really knotted ...

It means you are very confused about a worrying problem.

McClusky comes in. He can always tell if I need comforting. He brings his chewed squeaky-bone toy and drops it into my lap.

"No, McClusky. I can't give that to Mr. D. instead..."

And nothing seems to be happening about my party.

Has Mom forgotten?

Thursday

Lining up in the playground to go into class, Bradley is talking loudly to the other boy detectives.

"I am following a **very important lead** and we will *definitely* find the present TOMORROW!"
The others cheer and

punch the air

triumphantly.

In class we are putting the finishing touches to our **Ancient Egypt** display. Mr. D. brings something out of his desk that we weren't expecting: a small toy robot!

He tells us that a robot with a camera was sent into the Great Pyramid, along undiscovered corridors, to explore *unknown hidden chambers*.

I think about the secret hiding places inside the pyramids ...

And, while I'm thinking, I'm absent-mindedly twiddling the tiny pearl button in my pocket that I picked up in the hall ...

Why hadn't I thought of this before? It must be one of the buttons Nadia brought in for Mr. D.'s birthday present! What was it doing in the **Egypt** display?

A light bulb goes on ...

I have a

EUREKA MOMENT!

As soon as the bell goes for breaktime, Amy, Nadia, and Kirstie disappear to Choir practice but I RUSH across to the hall.

I lift the sugar-cube pyramid—and there, inside, is Mr. D.'s **missing birthday present!**

And what's this?
Half hidden
underneath I see a

FOOTBALL CAPTAIN badge. It must
have fallen off the culprit's sweater!
But a RED badge, not yellow and blue!

It was **BRADLEY**
who **hid the present!**

I pop the present under my sweater
for safekeeping and hurry out into
the playground to wait for the other
girl detectives, so I can tell them
what has happened.

"Bradley has known all along where it was because *he* put it there!" I say. "When he said I had **glittery** hands, he was trying to **distract us** by

BLAMING ME!"

"He must have planted the sequins as a false trail to send us in the wrong direction!" says Kirstie.

"It was one of your tiny pearl buttons that was the VITAL CLUE, Nadia," I say. "It must have fallen off the present when Bradley was hiding it."

We are SO relieved—but also MYSTIFIED. WHY did he hide it? We see Bradley across the playground, still looking confident and smiling.

"Should we say something?" asks Amy. "Tell the boys **we've won?**"

"And tell Bradley that we know it was *him*?" says Nadia.

But I say, "Bradley says he will find it tomorrow—let's see what he's planning first..."

EEK! I still don't have a costume for Egypt Day! Luckily I have some black cardboard, enough for one pair of Anubis ears for me and a smaller pair for McClusky.

I put Mr. D.'s present on my bedside table. There is

NO WAY

I am letting it out of my sight.

An idea is beginning to take shape in my head...

I think I've guessed what Bradley is up to, but I'm one step ahead of him.

Ah HA!

I know just what to do.

Friday

Me and McClusky put on our **Anubis ears** and we all set off.

Arriving at school to see all our class dressed up and looking

FANTASTIC!

There are two sphinxes, a hippo, *three* Cleopatras—Amy, Alisha, and Frankie—and ***somebody*** is disguised as the **Curse of the Mummy**, shuffling along trailing grubby bandages . . .

His face is covered and he doesn't speak, only groans, but his great height and birthday rosette make it pretty obvious who it is!

Joe has borrowed his mom's eyeliner.
"Egyptian boys wore make-up too,
you know!" he says, and he shows us
how to use it perfectly.

Instead of going to our classroom, we gather in the hall.

Mrs. Bagshott, the head teacher, comes in to admire our **Ancient Egypt** display.

"How splendid! WELL DONE!" she says.

We stand **proudly** next to our work and she takes our photograph.

! ! ! ! ! ! ! ! !

At that moment, Bradley steps
forward. He makes a big show of
lifting the pyramid, just as I expected.
But of course the present
ISN'T
THERE!

Bradley looks panicked
and horrified.
His **TA-DA** moment
has come to nothing.

I take the present out from under my sweater and give it to Mr. D. He is absolutely **over the moon.**

"I LOVE IT! THANK YOU, guys! You are *the best*!"

The girls' team high five each other. The rest of the boys' team are so glad to see Mr. D., so happy that they don't seem to care that we won and they lost, and they high five each other too! The whole class sings "Happy Birthday."

While everyone is distracted,
I confront Bradley.

"It was **YOU** all along!" I say.

Bradley just shrugs and turns to walk away.

I continue, **feeling angry**.

"You hid the present and then lied to us and pretended to *find* it yourself.

But WHY?"

He still doesn't answer, but he looks really upset.

"*Why*, Bradley?" I ask again, a bit more quietly this time.

"I thought people would like me if I was the **HERO** who saved the day," he says.

Now he looks so upset I think he might cry.

"You won't tell Mr. D.,

will you?"

I wonder if his confidence is mostly pretend and whether he has any real friends. I decide to let sleeping dogs lie, which means leaving things as they are and not stirring up trouble.

ZZZZzzzzzzz

I have a

GENIUS
idea.

When I tell Bradley, he thinks
it is genius too!

While Mr. D. is busy handing
out **mummy jelly sweets**,
I lend Bradley my second-best
glittery pen and he adds a message
to Mr. D.'s present.

Happy birthday, Mr. D!
I LOVE my new class.
From Bradley ☺

"Bradley," I say, "would you like to
come to my party on Sunday?"

Me and Beans sit together at lunch.
I tell him all about how my team
solved the case and he is
EXTREMELY impressed.

"I like it best when you and me are a
team, though," I say.

"ME TOO!" says Beans. "I only chose
Bradley because he seemed lonely."

I am so glad we are **BEST FRIENDS**
again.

"See you on Sunday at your party!"
all my friends are saying to me.

"Can't wait to know what the surprise
is!"

"Neither
can I!"

I think to myself.

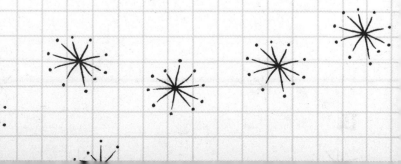

SATURDAY

I am
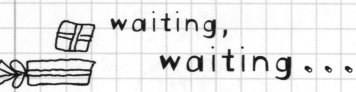
waiting,
    waiting,
        waiting...

I still don't know ANYTHING about
my birthday party.

Mom says, "Mum's the word!" and
laughs a lot at her own joke.

But it's no laughing matter—everyone will be arriving *tomorrow* at three o'clock, expecting a **fantastic surprise**; and no one will be more surprised than **me!**

Me and the twins are banished from the kitchen.

Mom tells the twins to **plump** up the cushions in the sitting room, and tells me to clean up McClusky's corner.

At bath time Mom insists that
McClusky has a bath too.

I give him an
extra brushing,
but he is *so* wiggly.
Why is he **SO** excited?

Snuggled down in bed, SO impatient
for my birthday to arrive.

I bet I will be awake

ALL NIGHT.

Sunday

I open my eyes.

Happy birthday to ME!

The kitchen looks amazing with polka-dot balloons, birthday garlands, and bunting everywhere. Mom is up already, having a cup of tea.

While she is giving me a big hug, McClusky and the twins come bowling in like a *tornado*.

Time to OPEN my presents!

The twins give me *FRED AND FLO'S FANTASTICALLY FAB STORYBOOK*, McClusky gives me some Dalmatian stickers, and Mom gives me a pair of new red sneakers—*exactly* the ones I was hoping for.

And *at last* it's time for my

PARTY!

As they arrive, each guest is given a colorful ticket that says ADMIT ONE, and they go through a red velvet curtain into the sitting room.

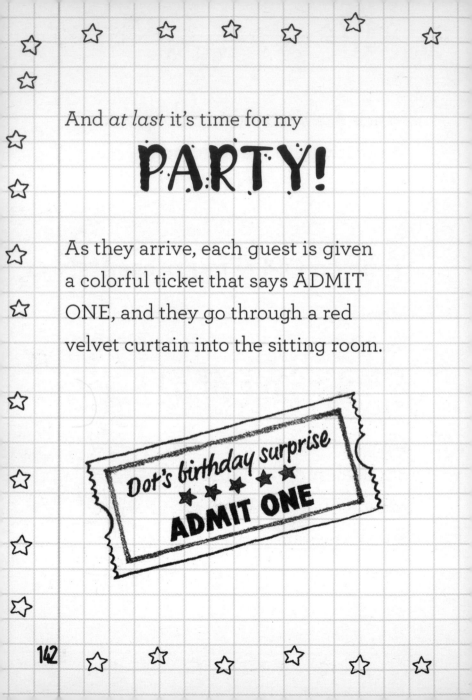

Dot's birthday surprise
★ ★ ★ ★
ADMIT ONE

Inside it is **very dark**, lit only with fairy lights around the room.

There are rows of comfy chairs and cushions on the floor.

Mom has transformed our sitting room into a

cinema!

She is giving out popcorn in polka-dot holders from the popcorn machine borrowed from school (so *that* was the big object under the sheet!).

We watch my new top-favorite **scary movie,** which is *Zombie Graveyard Ghouls.*

"Ha ha, Bradley," I say, "did you think it would be a *princess flower-fairy* kind of movie?" I nudge him jokily and he laughs.

When we have **screamed** halfway through, McClusky comes in with a basket of ice cream cups. He is wearing an old-time gold usherette's hat Mom has made for him (so *that's* why he had a little piece of gold thread on his ear!).

When it's finished, the BIGGEST surprise is Laura saying, "That was the best movie I have *ever* seen."

We play a few rounds of **Wink Murder** and **Who Am I?**, then a delicious party meal is delivered from Pink Vanilla, which is my very favorite café.

And best of all ...

Mom has made me *exactly* the birthday cake I wanted!

This has been the **best birthday EVER.**

Thank you SO MUCH, Mom!

The case of Mr. D.'s **missing birthday present**—solved.

What will our next tricky mystery be?

Have you read?

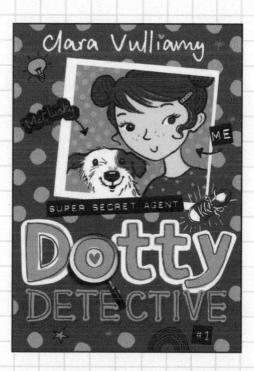

When someone seems set on sabotaging
the school show, Dot is determined to find
out how, and save the day!

When Dot starts hearing strange noises
at night, Beans is convinced there has to
be something SPOOKY afoot. But, before
they can be certain, Dot and Beans must
GET PROOF.

Dot and Beans can't wait for their school trip to Adventure Camp where they will do lots of exciting adventure activities and may even win the Adventurers' Prize! But why is someone trying to spoil the fun?

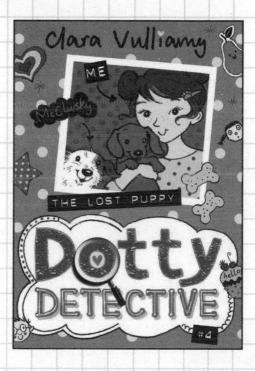

There's a fantastic surprise at the school
gates—Dot's friend Joe has brought along
his new sausage dog puppy, Chorizo!
She is SOOOOOO cute! But then she goes
missing. Can the Join the Dots Detectives
track down the lost little dog?

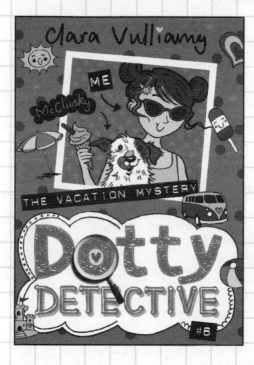

Join the gang on their next adventure as
Dot and her best friend, Beans, set off on
vacation. There are so many fun things to
do on the beach and at the campsite, but
eating doughnuts at the Nook café is their
favorite! So when things start mysteriously
disappearing from the Nook the Join the Dots
Detectives are determined to solve the case!

The end